# THE REV. W. AWDRY

# · MORE RAILWAY STORIES ·

## FEATURING THOMAS THE TANK ENGINE

TREASURE PRESS

The author gratefully acknowledges the ready help given by *Flying Scotman's* owner, Mr. A. F. PEGLER, and his assistant, Mr. E. HOYLE, in the preparation of this book.

# CONTENTS

# Troublesome Engines

## Henry and the Elephant

HENRY and Gordon were lonely when Thomas left the yard to run his Branch Line. They missed him very much.

They had more work to do. They couldn't wait in the shed till it was time, and find their coaches at the platform; they had to fetch them. They didn't like that.

Edward sometimes did odd jobs, and so did James, but James soon started grumbling too. The Fat Controller kindly gave Henry and Gordon new coats of paint (Henry chose green), but they still grumbled dreadfully.

"We get no rest, we get no rest," they complained as they clanked about the Yard; but the coaches only laughed.

"You're lazy and slack, you're lazy and slack," they answered in their quiet, rude way.

But when a Circus came to town, the engines forgot they were tired. They all wanted to shunt the special trucks and coaches.

They were dreadfully jealous of James when the Fat Controller told him to pull the train when the Circus went away.

However, they soon forgot about the animals as they had plenty of work to do.

One morning Henry was told to take some workmen to a tunnel which was blocked.

He grumbled away to find two trucks to carry the workmen and their tools.

"Pushing trucks! Pushing trucks!" he muttered in a sulky sort of way.

They stopped outside the tunnel, and tried to look through it, but it was quite dark; no daylight shone from the other end.

The workmen took their tools and went inside.

Suddenly with a shout they all ran out looking frightened.

"We went to the block and started to dig, but it grunted and moved," they said.

"Rubbish," said the foreman.

"It's not rubbish, it's big and alive; we're not going in there again."

"Right," said the foreman, "I'll ride in a truck and Henry shall push it out."

"Wheeeesh," said Henry unhappily. He hated tunnels (he had been shut up in one once), but this was worse; something big and alive was inside.

"Peep peep peep pip pip pee—eep!" he whistled, "I don't want to go in!"

"Neither do I," said his driver, "but we must clear the line."

"Oh dear! Oh dear!" puffed Henry as they slowly advanced into the darkness.

BUMP ————— !!!!

Henry's driver shut off steam at once.

"Help! Help! we're going back," wailed Henry, and slowly moving out into the daylight came first Henry, then the trucks, and last of all, pushing hard and rather cross, came a large elephant.

"Well I never did!" said the foreman. "It's an elephant from the Circus."

Henry's driver put on his brakes, and a man ran to telephone for the keeper.

The elephant stopped pushing and came towards them. They gave him some sandwiches and cake, so he forgot he was cross and remembered he was hungry. He drank three buckets of water without stopping, and was just going to drink another when Henry let off steam.

The elephant jumped, and "hoo——oosh", he squirted the water over Henry by mistake.

Poor Henry!

When the keeper came, the workmen rode home happily in the trucks, laughing at their adventure, but Henry was very cross.

"An elephant pushed me! an elephant hooshed me!" he hissed.

He was sulky all day, and his coaches had an uncomfortable time.

In the shed he told Gordon and James about the elephant, and I am sorry to say that instead of laughing and telling him not to be silly, they looked sad and said:

"You poor engine, you have been badly treated."

## Tenders and Turntables

THE BIG STATIONS at both ends of the line each have a turntable. The Fat Controller had them made so that Edward, Henry, Gordon and James can be turned round. It is dangerous for Tender Engines to go fast backwards. Tank Engines like Thomas don't need turntables; they can go just as well backwards as forwards.

But if you had heard Gordon talking a short while ago, you would have thought that the Fat Controller had given him a tender just to show how important he was.

"You don't understand, little Thomas," said Gordon, "we Tender Engines have a position to keep up. You haven't a Tender and that makes a difference. It doesn't matter where *you* go, but We are Important, and for the Fat Controller to make us shunt trucks, fetch coaches, and go on some of those dirty sidings it's —— it's —— well it's not the Proper Thing."

And Gordon puffed away in a dignified manner.

Thomas chuckled and went off with Annie and Clarabel.

Arrived at the Terminus, Gordon waited till all the passengers had got out; then, groaning and grumbling, he shunted the coaches to another platform.

"Disgraceful! Disgraceful!" he hissed as he ran backwards to the turntable.

The turntable was in a windy place close to the sea. It was only just big enough for Gordon, and if he was not on it just right, he put it out of balance, and made it difficult to turn.

Today, Gordon was in a bad temper, and the wind was blowing fiercely.

His Driver tried to make him stop in the right place; backwards and forwards they went, but Gordon wasn't trying.

At last Gordon's Driver gave it up. The Fireman tried to turn the handle, but Gordon's weight and the strong wind prevented him. The Driver, some platelayers, and the Fireman all tried together.

"It's no good," they said at last, mopping their faces, "your tender upsets the balance. If you were a nice Tank Engine, you'd be all right. Now you'll have to pull the next train backwards."

Gordon came to the platform. Some little boys shouted, "Come on quick, here's a new Tank Engine."

"What a swiz!" they said, when they came near, "it's only Gordon, back to front."

Gordon hissed emotionally.

He puffed to the junction. "Hullo!" called Thomas, "playing Tank Engines? Sensible engine! Take my advice, scrap your tender and have a nice bunker instead."

Gordon snorted, but didn't answer. Even James laughed when he saw him. "Take care," hissed Gordon, "you might stick too."

"No fear," chuckled James, "I'm not so fat as you."

"I mustn't stick," thought James anxiously, as he ran to the turntable later. He stopped on just the right place to balance the table. It could now swing easily. His fireman turned the handle ... James turned ... much too easily! The wind puffed him round like a top. He couldn't stop! ...

At last the wind died down, and James stopped turning, but not before Gordon, who had been turned on the loop line, had seen him.

"Well! Well!" he said, "are you playing round-abouts?"

Poor James, feeling quite giddy, rolled off to the shed without a word.

That night the three engines had an "indignation meeting".

"It's shameful to treat Tender Engines like this! Henry gets 'hooshed' by elephants; Gordon has to backwards and people think he's a Tank Engine. James spins round like a top, and everyone laughs at us. And added to that, the Fat Controller makes us shunt in dirty sidings. Ugh ——— ! !" said all three engines together.

"Listen," said Gordon ... He whispered something to the others: "We'll do it tomorrow. The Fat Controller *will* look silly!"

## Trouble in the Shed

THE FAT CONTROLLER sat in his office and listened. The Fat Controller frowned and said, "What a nuisance passengers are! How can I work with all this noise?"

The Station Master knocked and came in, looking worried.

"There's trouble in the shed, Sir. Henry is sulking; there is no train, and the Passengers are saying this is a Bad Railway."

"Indeed!" said the Fat Controller. "We cannot allow that. Will you quieten the passengers, please; I will go and speak to Henry."

He found Henry, Gordon and James looking sulky.

"Come along, Henry," he said, "it is time your train was ready."

"Henry's not going," said Gordon rudely. "We *won't* shunt like Common Tank Engines. We are Important Tender Engines. You fetch our coaches and we will pull them. Tender Engines don't shunt," and all three engines let off steam in a cheeky way.

"Oh indeed," said the Fat Controller severely. "We'll see about that; engines on My Railway do as they are told."

He hurried away, climbed into his car and drove to find Edward.

"The Yard has never been the same since Thomas left," he thought sadly.

Edward was shunting.

"Leave those trucks please, Edward; I want you to push coaches for me in the Yard."

"Thank you, Sir, that will be a nice change."

"That's a good engine," said the Fat Controller kindly, "off you go then."

So Edward found coaches for the three engines, and that day the trains ran as usual.

But when the Fat Controller came next morning, Edward looked unhappy.

Gordon came clanking past, hissing rudely. "Bless me!" said the Fat Controller. "What a noise!"

"They all hiss me, Sir," answered Edward sadly,. "They say 'Tender Engines don't shunt', and last night they said I had black wheels. I haven't, have I sir?"

"No, Edward, you have nice blue ones, and I'm proud of you. Tender Engines do shunt, but all the same you'd be happier in your own Yard. We need a Tank Engine here."

He went to an Engine Workshop, and they showed him all sorts of Tank Engines. There were big ones, and little ones; some looked happy, and some sad, and some looked at him anxiously, hoping he would choose them.

At last he saw a smart little green engine with four wheels.

"That's the one," he thought.

"If I choose you, will you work hard?"

"Oh Sir! Yes Sir!"

"That's a good engine; I'll call you Percy."

"Yes Sir! Thank you Sir!" said Percy happily.

So he bought Percy and drove him back to the Yard.

"Edward," he called, "here's Percy; will you show him everything?"

Percy soon learned what he had to do, and they had a happy afternoon.

Once Henry came by hissing as usual.

"Whee —— eesh!" said Percy suddenly; Henry jumped and ran back to the shed.

"How beautifully you wheeshed him," laughed Edward. "I can't wheesh like that."

"Oh!" said Percy modestly, "that's nothing; you should hear them in the workshop. You have to wheesh loudly to make yourself heard."

Next morning Thomas arrived. "The Fat Controller sent for me; I expect he wants help," he said importantly to Edward.

"Sh! Sh! here he comes."

Well done Thomas; you've been quick. Listen, Henry, Gordon and James are sulking; they say they won't shunt like Common Tank Engines. So I have shut them up, and I want you both to run the line."

"Common Tank Engines indeed!" snorted Thomas. "We'll show them."

"And Percy here will help too,' said the Fat Controller.

"Oh Sir! Yes Sir! Please Sir!" answered Percy excitedly.

Edward and Thomas worked the line. Starting at opposite ends, they pulled the trains, whistling cheerfully to each other as they passed.

Percy sometimes puffed along the Branch Line. Thomas was anxious, but both Driver and Guard promised to take care of Annie and Clarabel.

There were fewer trains, but the Passengers didn't mind; they knew the three other engines were having a Lesson.

Henry, Gordon and James stayed shut in the shed, and were cold, lonely and miserable. They wished now they hadn't been so silly.

## Percy runs away

Henry, Gordon and James were shut up for several days. At last the Fat Controller opened the shed.

"I hope you are sorry," he said sternly, "and understand you are not so important after all. Thomas, Edward and Percy have worked the Line very nicely. They need a change, and I will let you out if you promise to be good."

"Yes Sir!" said the three engines, "we will."

"That's right, but please remember that this 'no shunting' nonsense must stop."

He told Edward, Thomas and Percy that they could go and play on the Branch Line for a few days.

They ran off happily and found Annie and Clarabel at the Junction. The two coaches were so pleased to see Thomas again, and he took them for a run at once. Edward and Percy played with trucks.

"Stop! Stop! Stop!" screamed the trucks as they were pushed into their proper sidings, but the two engines laughed and went on shunting till the trucks were tidily arranged.

Next, Edward took some empty trucks to the Quarry, and Percy was left alone.

Percy didn't mind a bit; he liked watching trains and being cheeky to the engines.

"Hurry! Hurry! Hurry!" he would call to them. Gordon, Henry and James got very cross!

After a while he took some trucks over the main line to another siding. When they were tidy, he ran on to the main line again, and waited for the signalman to set the points so that he could cross back to the Yard.

Edward had warned Percy: "Be careful on the Main Line; whistle to tell the signalman you are there."

But Percy didn't remember to whistle, and the signalman was so busy, and forgot Percy.

Bells rang in the signal box; the man answered, saying the line was clear, and set the signals for the next train.

Percy waited and waited; the points were still against him. He looked along the Main Line . . . "Peep! Peep!" he whistled in horror for, rushing straight towards him, was Gordon with the Express.

"Poop poop poo-poo-poop!" whistled Gordon. His Driver shut off steam and applied the brakes.

Percy's Driver turned on full steam. "Back Percy! Back!" he urged; but Percy's wheels wouldn't turn quickly. Gordon was coming so fast that it seemed he couldn't stop. With shut eyes Percy waited for the crash. His Driver and Fireman jumped out.

"Oo —— ooh e —— er!" groaned Gordon. "Get out of my way."

Percy opened his eyes; Gordon had stopped with Percy's buffers a few inches from his own.

But Percy had begun to move. "I—won't stay — here — I'll — run — a — way," he puffed. He was soon clear of the station and running as fast as he could. He went through Edward's station whistling loudly, and was so frightened that he ran right up Gordon's hill without stopping.

He was tired then, and wanted to stop, but he couldn't . . . he had no Driver to shut off steam and to apply the brakes.

"I shall have to run till my wheels wear out," he thought sadly. "Oh dear! Oh dear!"

"I — want — to — stop, I — want — to — stop," he puffed in a tired sort of way.

He passed another signal box. "I know just what you want, little Percy," called the man kindly. He set the points and Percy puffed wearily on to a nice empty siding ending in a big bank of earth.

Percy was too tired now to care where he went. "I — want — to — stop, I — want — to — stop —— I — *have* — stopped!" he puffed thankfully, as his bunker buried itself in the bank.

"Never mind, Percy," said the workmen as they dug him out, "you shall have a drink and some coal, and then you'll feel better."

Presently Gordon arrived.

"Well done Percy, you started so quickly that you stopped a nasty accident."

"I'm sorry I was cheeky," said Percy, "you were clever to stop."

Percy now works in the Yard and finds coaches for the trains. He is still cheeky because he is that sort of engine, but is always *most* careful when he goes on the Main Line.

# PERCY the Small Engine

## Percy and the Signal

ERCY is a little green tank-engine who works in the Yard at the Big Station. He is a funny little engine, and loves playing jokes. These jokes sometimes get him into trouble.

"Peep peep!" he whistled one morning. "Hurry up, Gordon! the train's ready."

Gordon thought he was late and came puffing out.

"Ha ha!" laughed Percy, and showed him a train of dirty coal trucks.

Gordon didn't go back to the shed.

He stayed on a siding thinking how to pay Percy out.

"Stay in the Shed today," squeaked Percy to James. "The Fat Controller will come and see you."

James was a conceited engine. "Ah!" he thought, "the Fat Controller knows I'm a fine engine, ready for anything. He wants me to pull a Special Train."

So James stayed where he was, and nothing his Driver and Fireman could do would make him move.

But the Fat Controller never came, and the other engines grumbled dreadfully.

They had to do James' work as well as their own.

At last an Inspector came. 'Show a wheel, James," he said crossly. "You can't stay here all day."

"The Fat Controller told me to stay here," answered James sulkily. "He sent a message this morning."

"He did not," retorted the Inspector. "How could he? He's away for a week."

"Oh!" said James. "Oh!" and he came quickly out of the Shed. "Where's Percy?" Percy had wisely disappeared!

When the Fat Controller came back, he *did* see James, and Percy too. Both engines wished he hadn't!

James and Gordon wanted to pay Percy out; but Percy kept out of their way. One morning, however, he was so excited that he forgot to be careful.

"I say, you engines," he bubbled, "I'm to take some trucks to Thomas' Junction. The Fat Controller chose me specially. He must know I'm a Really Useful Engine."

"More likely he wants you out of the way," grunted James.

But Gordon gave James a wink. . . . Like this.

"Ah yes," said James, "just so. . . . You were saying, Gordon . . .?"

"James and I were just speaking about signals at the Junction. We can't be too careful about signals. But then, I needn't say that to a Really Useful Engine like you Percy."

Percy felt flattered.

"Of course not," he said.

"We had spoken of 'backing signals'," put in James. "They need extra special care, you know. Would you like me to explain?"

"No thank you, James," said Percy airily. "I know all about signals," and he bustled off importantly.

James and Gordon solemnly exchanged winks!

Percy was a little worried as he set out.

"I wonder what 'backing signals' are?" he thought.

"Never mind, I'll manage. I know all about signals." He puffed crossly to his trucks, and felt better.

He saw a signal just outside the Station. "Bother!" he said "It's at 'danger'."

"Oh! Oh! Oh!" screamed the trucks as they bumped into each other.

Presently the signal moved to show "line clear". Its arm moved up instead of down. Percy had never seen that sort of signal before. He was surprised.

" 'Down' means 'go'," he thought, "and 'up' means 'stop', so 'upper still' must mean 'go back'. I know! it's one of those 'backing signals'. How clever of me to find that out."

"Come on, Percy," said his Driver, "off we go."

But Percy wouldn't go forward, and his Driver had to let him "back" in order to start at all.

"I am clever," thought Percy, "even my Driver doesn't know about 'backing signals'," and he started so suddenly that the trucks screamed again.

"Whoah! Percy," called his Driver. "Stop! You're going the wrong way."

"But it's a 'backing signal'," Percy protested, and told him about Gordon and James. The Driver laughed, and explained about signals that point up.

"Oh dear!" said Percy, "let's start quickly before they come and see us."

But he was too late. Gordon swept by with the Express, and saw everything.

The big engines talked about signals that night. They thought the subject was funny. They laughed a lot. Percy thought they were being very silly!

## Duck Takes Charge

"DO you know what?" asked Percy.
"What?" grunted Gordon.

"Do you know what?"

"Silly," said Gordon crossly, "of course I don't know what, if you don't tell me what what is."

"The Fat Controller says that the work in the Yard is too heavy for me. He's getting a bigger engine to help me."

"Rubbish!" put in James. "Any engine could do it," he went on grandly. "If you worked more and chattered less, this Yard would be a sweeter, a better, and a happier place."

Percy went off to fetch some coaches.

"That stupid old signal," he thought, "no one listens to me now. They think I'm a silly little engine, and order me about.

"I'll show them! I'll show them!" he puffed as he ran about the Yard. But he didn't know how.

Things went wrong, the coaches and trucks behaved badly and by the end of the afternoon he felt tired and unhappy.

He brought some coaches to the Station, and stood panting at the end of the platform.

"Hullo Percy!" said the Fat Controller, "you look tired."

"Yes, Sir, I am, Sir; I don't know if I'm standing on my dome or my wheels."

"You look the right way up to me," laughed the Fat Controller. "Cheer up! The new engine is bigger than you, and can probably do the work alone. Would you like to help build my new harbour at Thomas' Junction? Thomas and Toby will help; but I need an engine there all the time."

"Oh yes, Sir, thank you Sir! said Percy happily.

The new engine arrived next morning.

"What is your name?" asked the Fat Controller kindly.

"Montague, Sir; but I'm usually called 'Duck'. They say I waddle; I don't really, Sir, but I like 'Duck' better than Montague."

"Good!" said the Fat Controller. " 'Duck' it shall be. Here Percy, come and show 'Duck' round."

The two engines went off together. At first the trucks played tricks, but soon found that playing tricks on Duck was a mistake! The coaches behaved well, though James, Gordon and Henry did not.

They watched Duck quietly doing his work. "He seems a simple sort of engine," they whispered, "we'll have some fun.

"Quaa-aa-aak! Quaa-aa-aak!" they wheezed as they passed him.

Percy was cross; but Duck took no notice. "They'll get tired of it soon," he said.

Presently the three engines began to order Duck about.

Duck stopped. "Do they tell you to do things, Percy?" he asked.

"Yes they do," answered Percy sadly.

"Right," said Duck, "we'll soon stop *that* nonsense."

He whispered something. . . . "We'll do it tonight."

The Fat Controller had had a good day. There had been no grumbling passengers, all the trains had run to time, and Duck had worked well in the Yard.

The Fat Controller was looking forward to hot buttered toast for tea at home.

He had just left the office when he heard an extraordinary noise. "Bother!" he said, and hurried to the Yard.

Henry, Gordon and James were Wheeeeeshing and snorting furiously; while Duck and Percy calmly sat on the points outside the Shed, refusing to let the engines in.

"STOP THAT NOISE," he bellowed.

"Now Gordon."

"They won't let us in," hissed the big engine crossly.

"Duck, explain this behaviour."

"Beg pardon, Sir, but I'm a Great Western Engine. We Great Western Engines do our work without Fuss; but we are *not* ordered about by other engines. You, Sir, are our Controller. We will of course move if you order us; but, begging your pardon, Sir, Percy and I would be glad if you would inform these—er—engines that we only take orders from you."

The three big engines hissed angrily.

"SILENCE!" snapped the Fat Controller. "Percy and Duck, I am pleased with your work today; but *not* with your behaviour tonight. You have caused a Disturbance."

Gordon, Henry and James sniggered. They stopped suddenly when the Fat Controller turned on them. "As for you," he thundered, "you've been worse. You made the Disturbance. Duck is quite right. This is My Railway, and I give the orders."

When Percy went away, Duck was left to manage alone.

He did so . . . easily!

## Percy and Harold

PERCY worked hard at the Harbour. Toby helped, but sometimes the loads of stone were too heavy, and Percy had to fetch them for himself. Then he would push the trucks along the quay to where the workmen needed the stone for their building.

An airfield was close by, and Percy heard the aeroplanes zooming overhead all day. The noisiest of all was a helicopter, which hovered, buzzing like an angry bee.

"Stupid thing!" said Percy, "why can't it go and buzz somewhere else?"

One day Percy stopped near the airfield. The helicopter was standing quite close.

"Hullo!" said Percy, "who are you?"

"I'm Harold, who are you?"

"I'm Percy. What whirly great arms you've got."

"They're nice arms," said Harold, offended. "I can hover like a bird. Don't you wish *you* could hover?"

"Certainly not; I like my rails, thank you."

"I think railways are slow," said Harold in a bored voice. "They're not much use, and quite out of date." He whirled his arms and buzzed away.

Percy found Toby at the Top Station arranging trucks.

"I say, Toby," he burst out, "that Harold, that stuck-up whirlibird thing, says I'm slow and out of date. Just let him wait, I'll show him!"

He collected his trucks and started off, still fuming.

Soon above the clatter of the trucks they heard a familiar buzzing.

"Percy," whispered his Driver, "there's Harold. He's not far ahead. Let's race him."

"Yes, let's," said Percy excitedly, and quickly gathering speed, he shot off down the line.

The Guard's wife had given him a flask of tea for "elevenses". He had just poured out a cup when the Van lurched and he split it down his uniform. He wiped up the mess with his handkerchief, and staggered to the front platform.

Percy was pounding along, the trucks screamed and swayed, while the Van rolled and pitched like a ship at sea.

"Well, 'I'll be ding-dong-danged!" said the Guard.

Then he saw Harold buzzing alongside, and understood.

"Go it, Percy!" he yelled. "You're gaining."

Percy had never been allowed to run fast before; he was having the time of his life!

"Hurry! Hurry! Hurry!" he panted to the trucks.

"We-don't-want-to; we-don't-want-to," they grumbled; but it was no use, Percy was bucketing along with flying wheels, and Harold was high and alongside.

The Fireman shovelled for dear life, while the Driver was so excited he could hardly keep still.

"Well done, Percy," he shouted, "we're gaining! We're going ahead! Oh good boy, good boy!"

Far ahead, a "distant signal" warned them that the Wharf was near. Shut off steam, whistle, "Peep, peep, peep, brakes, Guard, please." Using Percy's brakes too, the Driver carefully checked the train's headlong speed. They rolled under the main line, and halted smoothly on the Wharf.

"Oh dear!" groaned Percy, "I'm sure we've lost."

The Fireman scrambled to the cab roof. "We've won! we've won!" he shouted and nearly fell off in his excitement.

"Harold's still hovering. He's looking for a place to land!"

"Listen boys!" the Fireman called. "Here's a song for Percy."

Said Harold helicopter to our Percy, "You are slow!
Your Railway is out of date and not much use, you know."
But Percy, with his stone-trucks, did the trip in record time;
And we beat that helicopter on Our Old Branch Line.

The Driver and Guard soon caught the tune, and so did the workmen on the quay.

Percy loved it. "Oh thank you!" he said. He liked the last line best of all.

## Percy's Promise

A MOB of excited children poured out of Annie and Clarabel one morning, and raced down to the beach.

"They're the Vicar's Sunday School," explained Thomas "I'm busy this evening, but the Station-master says I can ask you to take them home."

"Of course I will," promised Percy.

The children had a lovely day. But at teatime it got very hot. Dark clouds loomed overhead. Then came lightning, thunder, and rain. The children only just managed to reach shelter before the deluge began.

Annie and Clarabel stood at the platform. The children scrambled in.

"Can we go home please, Station-master?" asked the Vicar.

The Station-master called Percy. "Take the children home quickly please," he ordered.

The rain streamed down on Percy's boiler. "Ugh!" he shivered, and thought of his nice dry shed. Then he remembered.

"A promise is a promise," he told himself, "so here goes."

His Driver was anxious. The river was rising fast. It foamed and swirled fiercely, threatening to flood the country any minute.

The rain beat in Percy's face. "I wish I could see, I wish I could see," he complained.

They left a cutting, and found themselves in water. "Oooh my wheels!" shivered Percy. "It's cold!" but he struggled on.

"Oooooooooooooooshshshshshsh!" he hissed, "it's sloshing my fire."

They stopped and backed the coaches to the cutting and waited while the Guard found a telephone.

He returned looking gloomy.

"We couldn't go back if we wanted," he said, "the bridge near the Junction is down."

The Fireman went to the Guard's Van carrying a hatchet.

"Hullo!' said the Guard, "you look fierce."

"I want some dry wood for Percy's fire, please."

They broke up some boxes, but that did not satisfy the Fireman. "I'll have some of your floor boards," he said.

"What! my nice floor," grumbled the Guard. "I only swept it this morning," but he found a hatchet and helped.

Soon they had plenty of wood stored in Percy's bunker. His fire burnt well now. He felt warm and comfortable again.

"Buzzzzzzzzzzzzzzzzzzzzzz! Buzzzzzzzzzzzzzzzzzzzzzz! Buzzzzzzzzzzzzzzzzzzzzzz!"

"Oh dear!" thought Percy sadly, "Harold's come to laugh at me."

Bump! Something thudded on Percy's boiler. "Ow!" he exclaimed in a muffled voice, "that's really too bad! He needn't *throw* things."

His driver unwound a parachute from Percy's indignant front.

"Harold isn't throwing things at you," he laughed, "he's dropping hot drinks for us."

They all had a drink of cocoa, and felt better.

Percy had steam up now. "Peep peep! Thank you, Harold!" he whistled. "Come on, let's go."

The water lapped his wheels. "Ugh!" he shivered. It crept up and up and up. It reached his ash-pan, then it sloshed at the fire. "Ooooooooooooooshshshshshshsh-shshshshsh!"

Percy was losing steam; but he plunged bravely on. "I promised," he panted, "I promised."

They piled his fire high with wood, and managed to keep him steaming.

"I *must* do it," he gasped, "I must, I must, I must."

He made a last great effort, and stood, exhausted but triumphant, on rails which were clear of the flood.

He rested to get steam back, then brought the train home.

"Three cheers for Percy!" called the Vicar, and the children nearly raised the roof!

The Fat Controller arrived in Harold. First he thanked the men. "Harold told me you were—er—wizard, Percy. He says he can beat you at some things . . ."

Percy snorted.

" . . . but *not* at being a submarine." He chuckled. "I don't know what you've both been playing at, and I won't ask! But I do know that you're a Really Useful Engine."

"Oh Sir!" whispered Percy happily.

# Duck and the Diesel Engine

## Domeless Engines

A SPECIAL train arrived one day, and the Fat Controller welcomed the passengers. They looked at everything in the Yard, and photographed the engines. Duck's Driver let some of them ride in his cab.

"They're the Railway Society," his Driver explained. "they've come to see us. Their engine's 'City of Truro'. He was the first to go 100 miles an hour. Let's get finished, then we can go and talk to him."

"Oh!" said Duck, awed. "He's too famous to notice me."

"Rubbish!" smiled his Driver. "Come on."

Duck found "City of Truro" at the coaling stage.

"May I talk to you?" he asked shyly.

"Of course," smiled the famous engine, "I see you are one of Us."

"I try to teach them Our ways," said Duck modestly.

"All ship-shape and Swindon fashion. That's right."

"Please, could you tell me how you beat the South Western?"

So "City of Truro" told Duck all about his famous run from Plymouth to Bristol more than fifty years ago. They were soon firm friends, and talked "Great Western" till late at night.

"City of Truro" left early next morning.

"Good riddance!" grumbled Gordon. "Chattering all night keeping important engines awake! Who *is* he anyway?"

"He's 'City of Truro'. He's famous."

"As famous as me? Nonsense!"

"He's famouser than you. He went 100 miles an hour before you were drawn or thought of."

"So he says; but I didn't like his looks. *He's got no dome*," said Gordon darkly. "Never trust domeless engines, they're not respectable.

"I never boast," Gordon continued modestly; "but 100 miles an hour would be easy for me. Goodbye!"

Presently Duck took some trucks to Edward's station. He was cross, and it was lucky for those trucks that they tried no tricks.

"Hullo!" called Edward. "The famous 'City of Truro' came through this morning. He whistled to me; wasn't he kind?"

"He's the finest engine in the world," said Duck, and he told Edward about "City of Truro", and what Gordon had said.

"Don't take any notice," soothed Edward, "he's just jealous. He thinks no engine should be famous but him. Look! He's coming now."

Gordon's boiler seemed to have swollen larger than ever. He was running very fast. He swayed up and down and from side to side as his wheels pounded the rails.

"He did it! I'll do it! He did it! I'll do it!" he panted. His train rocketed past and was gone.

Edward chuckled and winked at Duck. "Gordon's trying do a 'City of Truro'," he said.

Duck was still cross. "I should think he'll knock himself to bits," he snorted. "I heard something rattle as he went through."

Gordon's Driver eased him off. "Steady boy!" he said. "We aren't running a race."

"We are then," said Gordon; but he said it to himself.

"I've never known him ride so roughly before." remarked his Driver.

His Fireman grabbed the brake handle to steady himself. "He's giving himself a hammering, and no mistake."

Soon Gordon began to feel a little queer. "The top of my boiler seems funny," he thought; "it's just as if something was loose. I'd better go slower."

But by then it was too late!

They met the wind on the viaduct. It wasn't just a gentle wind; nor was it a hard steady wind. It was a teasing wind which blew suddenly in hard puffs, and caught out unawares.

Gordon thought it wanted to push him off the bridge. "No you don't!" he said firmly.

But the wind had other ideas. It curled round his boiler, crept under his loose dome, and lifted it off and away into the valley below. It fell on the rocks with a clang.

Gordon was most uncomfortable. He felt cold where his dome wasn't, and besides, people laughed at him as he passed.

At the Big Station, he tried to "Wheeeesh" them away; but they crowded round no matter what he did.

On the way back, he wanted his driver to stop and find his dome, and was very cross when he wouldn't.

He hoped the shed would be empty; but all the engines were there waiting.

"Never trust domeless engines," said a voice. "They aren't respectable."

## Pop Goes the Diesel

"CITY OF TRURO'S" visit made Duck very proud of being Great Western. He talked endlessly about it. But he worked hard too and made everything go like clockwork.

The trucks behaved well, the coaches were ready on time, and the passengers even stopped grumbling!

But the engines didn't like having to bustle about. "There are two ways of doing things," Duck told them, "the Great Western way, or the wrong way. I'm Great Wesern and . . ."

"Don't we know it!" they groaned. They were glad when a visitor came.

The visitor purred smoothly towards them. The Fat Controller climbed down. "Here is Diesel," he said, "I have agreed to give him a trial. He needs to learn. Please teach him, Duck."

"Good morning," purred Diesel in an oily voice, "pleased to meet you, Duck. Is that James?—*and* Henry?—*and* Gordon too? I am delighted to meet such famous engines." And he purred towards them.

The silly engines were flattered. "He has very good manners," they murmured, "we are pleased to have him in our Yard."

Duck had his doubts.

"Come on!" he said shortly.

"Ah! yes!" said Diesel, "The Yard, of course. Excuse me, engines," and he purred after Duck, talking hard. "Your worthy Fat . . ."

"Sir Topham Hatt to you," ordered Duck.

Diesel looked hurt. "Your worthy Sir Topham Hatt thinks I need to learn. He is mistaken. We Diesels don't need to learn. We know everything. We come to a yard and improve it. We are revolutionary."

"Oh!" said Duck, "If you're revo-thingummy, perhaps you would collect my trucks, while I fetch Gordon's coaches."

Diesel, delighted to show off, purred away. With much banging and clashing he collected a row of trucks. Duck left Gordon's coaches in the Station and came back.

Diesel was not trying to take some trucks from a siding nearby. They were old and empty. Clearly they had not been touched for a long time.

Their brakes would not come off properly. Diesel found them hard to move.

Pull—Push—Backwards—Forwards.    "Oheeeer! Oheeeer!" the trucks groaned. "We can't! We *won't!*"

Duck watched the operation with interest.

Diesel lost patience. "GrrrrrRRRRRrrrrrRRRRR!" he roared, and gave a great heave. The trucks jerked forward.

"Oher! Oher!" they screamed. "We *can't!* We *WON'T!*" Some of their brakes broke, and the gear hanging down bumped on the rails and sleepers.

"WE CAN'T! WE WON'T! Aaaah!" Their trailing brakes caught in the points and locked themselves solid.

"GrrrrrRRRRRrrrrrRRRRRRrrrrrRRRRR!" roared Diesel; a rusty coupling broke, and he shot forward suddenly by himself.

"Ho! Ho! Ho!" chuckled Duck.

Diesel recovered and tried to push the trucks back; but they wouldn't move, and he had to give up. Duck ran quietly round to where the other trucks all stood in line. "Thank you for arranging these, Diesel," he said, "I must go now."

"Don't you want this lot?"

"No thank you."

Diesel gulped. "And I've taken all this trouble," he almost shrieked. "Why didn't you tell me?"

"You never asked me. Besides," said Duck innocently, "you were having such fun being revo-whatever-it-was-you-said. Goodbye."

Diesel had to help the workmen clear the mess. He hated it. All the trucks and coaches were laughing. Presently he heard them singing. Their song grew louder and louder, and soon it echoed through the Yard.

Trucks are waiting in the Yard; tackling them with ease'll
"Show the world what I can do," gaily boasts the Diesel.
In and out he creeps about, like a big black weasel.
When he pulls the wrong trucks out—Pop goes the Diesel!

"Gurrrrr!" he growled, and scuttling away, sulked in the Shed.

## Dirty Work

WHEN Duck returned, and heard the trucks singing, he was horrified. "Shut up!" he ordered, and bumped them hard. "I'm sorry our trucks were rude to you, Diesel," he said.

Diesel was still furious. "It's all your fault. You made them laugh at me," he complained.

"Nonsense," said Henry, "Duck would never do that. We engines have our differences; but we *never* talk about them to trucks. That would be des—des . . ."

"Disgraceful!" said Gordon.

"Disgusting!" put in James.

"Despicable!" finished Henry.

Diesel hated Duck. He wanted him to be sent away. So he made a plane.

Next day he spoke to the trucks. "I see you like jokes," he said in his oily voice. "You made a good joke about me yesterday. I laughed and laughed. Duck told me one about Gordon. I'll whisper it. . . . Don't tell Gordon I told you," and he sniggered away.

"Haw! haw! haw!" guffawed the trucks. "Gordon will be cross with Duck when he knows. Let's tell him and pay duck out for bumping us."

Diesel went to all the sidings, and in each he told different stories. He said Duck had told them to him. This was untrue; but the trucks didn't know.

They laughed rudely at the engines as they went by, and soon Gordon, Henry and James found out why.

"Disgraceful!" said Gordon.

"Disgusting!" said James.

"Despicable!" said Henry. "We cannot allow it."

They consulted together. "Yes," they said, "he did it to us. We'll do it to him, and see how *he* likes it."

Duck was tired out. The trucks had been cheeky and troublesome. He had had hard work to make them behave. He wanted a rest in the Shed.

"Hooooooooosh! KEEP OUT!" The three engines barred his way, and Diesel lurked behind.

"Stop fooling," said Duck, "I'm tired."

"So are we," hissed the engines. "We are tired of *you*. We like Diesel. We don't like you. You tell tales about us to trucks."

"I don't."

'You do.''

"I don't."

"You do."

The Fat Controller came to stop the noise.

"Duck called me a 'galloping sausage'," spluttered Gordon.

" . . . rusty red scrap-iron," hissed James.

" . . . I'm 'old square wheels'," fumed Henry.

"Well Duck?"

Duck considered. "I only wish Sir," he said gravely, "that I'd thought of those names myself. If the dome fits . . ."

"Ha! Ahem!" The Fat Controller coughed.

"He made trucks laugh at us," accused the engines.

The Fat Controller recovered. "Did you, Duck?"

"Certainly not Sir! No *steam* engine would be as mean as that."

"No Diesel, you heard what Duck said."

"I can't understand it Sir. To think that Duck of all engines . . . I'm dreadfully grieved Sir; but know nothing."

"I see." Diesel squirmed and hoped he didn't.

"I am sorry, Duck," the Fat Controller went on; 'but you must go to Edward's station for a while. I know he will be glad to see you."

"Beg pardon Sir, do you mean now?"

"Yes please."

"As you wish Sir," Duck trundled sadly away, while Diesel smirked with triumph in the darkness.

## A Close Shave

So Duck came to Edward's station.

"It's not fair," he complained, "Diesel has made the Fat Controller and all the engines think I'm horrid."

Edward smiled. "I know you aren't," he said "and so does the Fat Controller. You wait and see."

Duck felt happier with Edward. He helped him with his trucks and coaches, and sometimes helped foreign engines by pushing their trains up the hill.

But Gordon, Henry and James never spoke to him at all.

One day he pushed behind a goods train and helped it to the top.

"Peep peep! Goodbye! he called, and rolled gently over the crossing to the other line. Duck loved coasting down the hill, running easily with the wind whistling past. He hummed a little tune.

---

"Peeeeeep! Peeeeeep! Peeeeeeeep!"

"That sounds like a guard's whistle," he thought. "But we haven't a Guard."

His Driver heard it too, and looked back. "Hurry, Duck, hurry," he called urgently.

"There's been a break-away, some trucks are chasing us."

There were twenty heavily loaded trucks. "Hurrah! Hurrah! Hurrah!" they laughed, "We've broken away! We've broken away! We've broken away!" and before the signalman could change the points they followed Duck on to the down line.

"Chase him! Bump him! Throw him off the rails!" they yelled, and hurtled after Duck, bumping and swaying with ever-increasing speed.

The Guard saved Duck. Though the trucks had knocked him off his van, he got up and ran behind, blowing his whistle to attract the Driver's attention.

"Now what?" asked the Fireman.

"As fast as we can," said the Driver grimly, "then they'll catch us gradually."

They raced through Edward's station whistling furiously, but the trucks caught them with a shuddering jar. The Fireman climbed back, and the van brakes came on with a scream.

Braking carefully, the Driver was gaining control.

"Another clear mile and we'll do it," he said.

They swept round a bend.

"Oh glory! look at that!"

A passenger train was just pulling out on their line, from the station ahead.

The Driver leapt to his reverser; Hard over—Full steam—Whistle.

"It's up to you now, Duck," he said.

Duck put every ounce of weight and steam against the trucks.

They felt his strength. "On! On!" they yelled; but Duck was holding them now.

"I must stop them. I *must*."

The station came nearer and nearer. The last coach cleared the platform.

"It's too late," Duck groaned, and shut his eyes.

He felt a sudden swerve, and slid, shuddering and groaning along a siding.

A barber had set up shop in a wooden shed in the yard. He was shaving a customer.

There was a sliding groaning crash, and part of the wall caved in.

The customer jumped nervously; but the barber held him down. "It's only an engine." he said calmly, and went on lathering.

"Beg pardon Sir!" gasped Duck, "Excuse my intrusion."

"No. I won't," said the barber crossly, "you've frightened my customers and spoilt my new paint. I'll teach you." And he lathered Duck's face all over.

Poor Duck.

They were pulling the trucks away when the Fat Controller arrived. The Barber was telling the workmen what he thought.

"I do *not* like engines popping through my walls," he fumed. "They disturb my customers."

"I appreciate your feelings," said the Fat Controller, "and we'll gladly repair the damage; but you must know that this engine and his crew have prevented a serious accident. You and many others might have been badly hurt."

The Fat Controller paused impressively. "It was a very close shave," he said.

"Oh!" said the barber, "Oh! Excuse me." He ran into his shop, fetched a basin of water, and washed Duck's face.

"I'm sorry, Duck," he said. "I didn't know you were being a brave engine."

"That's all right, Sir," said Duck. "I didn't know that either."

"You were very brave indeed," said the Fat Controller kindly. "I'm proud of you. I shall tell 'City of Truro' about you next time he comes."

"Oh Sir!" Duck felt happier than he had been for weeks.

"And now," said the Fat Controller, "when you are mended you are coming home."

"Home Sir? Do you mean the Yard?"

"Of course."

"But Sir, they don't like me. They like Diesel."

"Not now." The Fat Controller smiled. "I never believed Diesel. After you went he told lies about Henry; so I sent him packing. The engines are sorry and want you back."

So, when a few days later he came home shining with new paint, there was a really rousing welcome for Duck the Great Western engine.

# Main Line Engines

## The Diseasel

BILL AND BEN are tank-engines who live at a port on Edward's line. Each has four wheels, a tiny chimney and dome, and a small squat cab.

They are kept busy pulling trucks for ships in the harbour and engines on the main line.

The trucks are filled with China Clay dug from the nearby hills. China Clay is important. It is needed for pottery, paper, paint, plastics, and many other things.

One morning they arranged some trucks and went away for more. They returned to find them all gone.

They were most surprised.

Their Drivers examined a patch of oil. "That's a diesel," they said, wiping the rails clean.

"It's a what'll?" asked Bill.

"A diseasel, I think," replied Ben. "There's a notice about them in our Shed."

"I remember, 'Coughs and sneezles spread diseasels.'"

"Who had a cough in his smokebox yesterday?"

"Fireman cleaned it, didn't he?"

"Yes, but the dust made him sneezle: so there you are. It's *your* fault the diseasel came."

"It isn't!"

"It is!"

"Stop arguing, you two," laughed their Drivers.

"Come on! Let's go and rescue our trucks."

Bill and Ben were aghast. "But he'll magic us away like the trucks."

Their Drivers laughed. "He won't magic us; we'll more likely magic him! Listen. He doesn't know you're twins; so we'll take your names and numbers off and then this is what we'll do . . ."

Bill and Ben chuckled with delight. "Come on! Let's go!" they said eagerly.

Creeping into Edward's Yard they found the diesel on a siding with the missing trucks. Ben hid behind, but Bill went boldly alongside and stood facing the diesel on the points leading out to the main line.

The diesel looked up. "Do you mind?" he asked.

"Yes," said Bill, "I do. I want my trucks please."

"These are mine," said the diesel. "Go away."

Bill pretended to be frightened. "You're a big bully," he whimpered. "You'll be sorry."

He moved over the points, ran back, and hid behind the trucks on the other side.

Ben now came forward. The diesel had to stop suddenly.

"Truck stealer," hissed Ben. He ran away too, and Bill took his place.

This went on and on till the diesel's eyes nearly popped out.

"Stop!" he begged. "You're making me giddy!"

The two engines gazed at him side by side. He shut his eyes. "Are there *two* of you?" he whispered.

"Yes, we're twins."

"I might have known it," he groaned.

Just then, Edward bustled up. "Bill and Ben, why are you playing here?"

"We're *not* playing," protested Bill.

"We're rescuing trucks," squeaked Ben.

"What do you mean?"

"Even *you* don't come in our Yard without asking."

"And you only take the trucks we give you."

"But," they both squeaked indignantly, "this diseasel didn't even ask. He just took the lot!"

"There is no cause to be rude," said Edward severely. "This engine is a 'Metropolitan-Vickers, diesel-electric, Type 2,'"

The twins were abashed. "We're sorry Mr-er. . . ."

"Never mind," he smiled, "call me BoCo. I'm sorry I didn't understand about the trucks."

"That's all right then," said Edward. "Off you go, Bill and Ben. Fetch BoCo's trucks, then you can take these."

The twins scampered away. Edward smiled.

"There's no real harm in them," he said, "but they're maddening at times."

BoCo chuckled. "Maddening," he said, "is the word."

### Buzz Buzz

BoCo reached the Big Station and arranged his trucks. Then he went to the Shed, and asked politely if he could come in.

Duck was not pleased to see a diesel but, presently, when he found that BoCo knew Edward, he became more friendly. And by the time BoCo had told him about Bill and Ben they were laughing together like old friends.

"Have they ever played tricks on *you*?" asked BoCo.

"Goodness me! Yes!" chuckled Duck. "Edward is the only one who can keep them in order."

"You know," went on Duck, "I sometimes call them 'The Bees'."

"A good name," chuckled BoCo. "They're terrors when they start buzzing round."

Just then James bustled in. "What's that, Duck? Are you terrified of bees? They're only insects after all: so don't let that buzz-box diesel tell you different."

"His name is BoCo, and he didn't. We ..."

"I wouldn't care," interrupted James, "if hundreds were swarming round. I'd just blow smoke and make them buzz off."

"Buzz Buzz Buzz," retorted Duck.

James retired into a huff.

James was to pull the Express next morning, and when Duck brought his coaches the platform was crowded.

"Mind your backs! MIND YOUR BACKS!" Two porters were taking a loaded trolley to the front van. Fred drove, while Bert walked behind.

"Careful, Fred! Careful!" warned Bert, but Fred was in a hurry and didn't listen.

Suddenly an old lady appeared in front.

Fred stopped dead, but the luggage slid forward and burst the lid of a large white wooden box.

Some bees flew out, and just as James came backing down, they began to explore the station.

Someone shouted a warning. The platform cleared like magic.

The bees were too sleepy to be cross. They found the empty station cold. James's Fireman was trying to couple the train. They buzzed round him hopefully. They wanted him to mend their hive. Then they could go back and be warm again.

But the Fireman didn't understand. He thought they would sting him.

He gave a yell, ran back to the cab and crouched with his jacket over his head.

The Driver didn't understand either. He swatted at the bees with the shovel.

The bees, disappointed, turned their attention to James.

James's boiler was nice and warm. The bees swarmed round it happily.

"Buzz off! BUZZ OFF!" he hissed. He made smoke, but the wind blew it away, and the bees stayed.

At last one settled on his hot smokebox. It burnt its feet. The bee thought James had stung it on purpose. It stung James back – right on the nose!

"Eeeeeeeeeeeeee!" whistled James. He had had enough: so had his Driver and Fireman. They started without waiting for the Guard's whistle.

They didn't notice till too late, that they'd left their train behind.

In the end it was BoCo who pulled the Express. He was worried at first about leaving his trucks, but Duck promised to look after them and so it was arranged. He managed to gain back some of the lost time, and the Fat Controller was pleased with him.

No one seemed to notice when James came back to the Shed. They were talking about a new kind of beehive on wheels. It was red, they said. Then they all said "Buzz, buzz, buzz," and laughed a lot.

James thought that for big Main Line Engines they were being very silly.

## Wrong Road

THOMAS'S BRANCH LINE is important, and so is Edward's. They both bring in valuable traffic, but their track and bridges are not so strong as those on the Main.

That is why the Fat Controller does not allow the heavier Main Line Engines such as Gordon and Henry to run on them.

If, however, you had heard Gordon talking to Edward a short while ago, you would have thought that the Fat Controller had forbidden him to run on Branch Lines for quite another reason.

"It's not fair," grumbled Gordon.

"What isn't fair?" asked Edward.

"Letting Branch Line diesels pull Main Line trains."

"Never mind, Gordon. I'm sure BoCo will let you pull his trucks sometimes. That would make it quite fair."

Gordon spluttered furiously. "I *won't* pull BoCo's dirty trucks. I *won't* run on Branch Lines."

"Why not? It would be a nice change."

"The Fat Controller would never approve," said Gordon loftily. "Branch Lines are vulgar."

He puffed away in a dignified manner. Edward chuckled and followed him to the Station . . .

Gordon, his Driver and his Fireman all say it was the lady's fault. She wore a green floppy hat, and was saying "Goodbye" to a friend sitting in the coach nearest the Guard's Van.

It was almost time to start. The Fireman looked back. He was new to the job. He couldn't see the Guard but he did see something green waving. He thought it was the flag.

"Right away, Mate," he called.

But the Guard had not waved his flag. When Gordon started he left some luggage, several indignant passengers and the Guard all standing on the platform.

Every evening two fast trains leave the Big Station within five minutes. The 6.25 is Gordon's for the Main Line. Edward's, at 6.30, runs along the Branch.

By the time Gordon had been brought back, Edward's train was overdue.

"You've missed your 'path', Gordon", said the Fat Controller, crossly. "Now we must clear Edward's train before you can start."

This should have put everything right with the least possible trouble; but Control at the Big Station made things worse. They forgot to warn the signalman at Edward's Junction about the change of plan.

It was dark by the time the trains reached the Junction, and you can guess what happened – Edward went through on the Main, while Gordon was switched to the Branch . . .

It took the Fat Controller several hours to sort out the tangle and pacify the passengers.

In the end Gordon was left, with his fire drawn, cold and cross on one of Edward's sidings.

Bill and Ben peeped into the Yard next morning. They wondered if BoCo had brought them some trucks. There were no trucks, but they didn't mind that.

Teasing Gordon, they thought, would be much better fun!

"What's that?" asked Bill loudly.

"Ssh!" whispered Ben. "It's Gordon."

"It *looks* like Gordon, but it can't be. Gordon *never* comes on Branch Lines. He thinks them vulgar."

Gordon pretended he hadn't heard.

"If it isn't Gordon," said Ben, "it's just a pile of old iron . . ."

". . . which we'd better take to the scrap-yard."

"No, Bill, this lot's useless for scrap. We'll take it to the harbour and dump it in the sea."

Gordon was alarmed. "I *am* Gordon. Stop! Stop!"

The twins paid no attention. Gordon shut his eyes and prepared for the worst.

The twins argued loudly and long. Bill favoured the scrapyard, while Ben said that the cutting up in such places was something cruel.

It would be kinder, he urged, to give these remains a quick end in the sea. Besides, he went on, they would make a lovely splash.

Gordon could not view either prospect with any enthusiasm.

Up to that time he had disapproved of diesels.

They were, he considered, ugly, smelly, and noisy; but when he opened his eyes and saw BoCo coming into the Yard, he thought him the most beautiful sight he had ever seen.

"BoCo my dear engine!" he gasped. "Save me!"

BoCo quickly sized up the situation, and sent Bill and Ben about their business.

They were cheeky at first, but BoCo threatened to take away the trucks of coal he had brought for them. That made them behave at once.

Gordon thought he was wonderful. "Those little demons!" he said. "How do you do it?"

"Ah well," said BoCo. "It's just a knack."

Gordon thinks to this day that BoCo saved his life; but we know that the twins were only teasing – don't we?

## Edward's Exploit

EDWARD scolded the twins severely, but told Gordon it served him right. Gordon was furious.

A few days later, some Enthusiasts came. On their last afternoon they went to the China Clay Works.

Edward found it hard to start the heavy train.

"Did you see him straining?" asked Henry.

"Positively painful," remarked James.

"Just pathetic," grunted Gordon. "He should give up and be Preserved before it's too late."

"Shut up!" burst out Duck. "You're all jealous. Edward's better than any of you."

"You're right, Duck," said BoCo. "Edward's old, but he'll surprise us all."

Bill and Ben were delighted with their visitors. They loved being photographed and took the party to the Workings in a "Brakevan Special".

On the way home, however, the weather changed. Wind and rain buffeted Edward. His sanding gear failed, his wheels slipped, and his Fireman rode in front dropping sand on the rails by hand.

"ComeOn-ComeOn-ComeOn," panted Edward breathlessly. "This is dreadful!"

But there was worse to come. Before his Driver could check them, his wheels slipped fiercely again and again.

With a shrieking crack, something broke and battered his frame and splashers up and out of shape.

The passengers gathered round while the Crew inspected the damage. Repairs took some time.

"One of your crank-pins broke, Edward," said his Driver at last. "We've taken your side-rods off. Now you're a 'single' like an old fashioned engine. Can you get these people home? They must start back tonight."

"I'll try, Sir," promised Edward.

They backed down to where the line was more nearly level. Edward puffed and pulled his hardest, but his wheels kept slipping and he just could not start the heavy train.

The passengers were getting anxious.

Driver, Fireman and Guard went along the train making adjustments between the coaches.

"We've loosened the couplings, Edward," they said. "Now you can pick your coaches up one by one, just as you do with trucks."

"That will be much easier," said Edward gratefully.

So, with the Fireman sanding carefully in front, the Driver gently opened the regulator.

Come . . . on! puffed Edward. He moved cautiously forward, ready to take the strain as his tender coupling tightened against the weight of the first coach.

The first coach moving, helped to start the second, the second helped the third, and so on down the train.

"I've done it! I've done it!" puffed Edward, his wheels spinning with excitement.

"Steady, Boy!" warned his Driver, skilfully checking the wheel-slip. "Well done, Boy!"

"You've got them! You've *got* them!" And he listened happily to Edward's steady beat as he forged slowly but surely up the hill.

The passengers were thrilled. Most had their heads out of windows. They waved and shouted, cheering Edward on.

The Fat Controller paced the platform. Henry with the Special train waited anxiously too.

They heard a 'Peep peep!" Then, battered, weary, but unbeaten, Edward steamed in.

The Fat Controller stepped angrily forward. He pointed to the clock, but excited passengers swept him aside. They cheered Edward, his Driver and Fireman to the echo, before rushing off to get in Henry's train.

Henry steamed away to another storm of cheers, but not before everyone knew Edward's story.

Edward went thankfully to the Shed, while Duck and BoCo saw to it that he was left in peace. Gordon and James remained respectfully silent.

The Fat Controller asked BoCo to look after Edward's line while he was being mended. BoCo was pleased. He worked well, and now they run it together. Bill and Ben still tease him, but BoCo doesn't mind.

He lives at Edward's Station, but is welcome any-where, for he is now one of the "family".

Donald and Douglas were the last to accept him, but he often helps with their goods trains, and the other day they were heard to remark, "For a diesel, yon BoCo's nae sich a bad sort of engine."

That, from the Caledonian Twins, is high praise indeed!

# Enterprising Engines

## Tenders for Henry

"I M not happy," complained Gordon.

"Your fire-box is out of order," said James. "No wonder, after all that coal you had yesterday."

"Hard work brings good appetite," snapped Gordon. "*You* wouldn't understand."

"I know," put in Duck, brightly. "It's boiler-ache. I warned you about that standpipe on the Other Railway; but you drank gallons."

"It's *not* boiler-ache," protested Gordon. "It's ..."

"Of course it is," said Henry. "That water's bad. It furs up your tubes. Your boiler must be full of sludge. Have a good wash-out. Then, you'll feel a different engine."

"Don't be vulgar," said Gordon huffily.

Gordon backed down on his train, hissing mournfully.

"Cheer up, Gordon!" said the Fat Controller.

'I can't, Sir. The others say I've got boiler-ache, but I haven't, Sir. I keep thinking about the Dreadful State of the World, Sir. Is it true, Sir, what the diesels, say?"

"What do they say?"

"They boast that they've *abolished Steam*, Sir."

"Yes, Gordon. It is true."

"What, Sir! All my Doncaster brothers, drawn the same time as me?"

"All gone, except one."

The Guard's whistle blew, and Gordon puffed sadly away.

"Poor old Gordon!" said the Fat Controller. "Hmm . . . If only we could! . . . Yes, I'll ask his Owner at once." He hurried away.

Arrangements took time, but one evening, Gordon's Driver ran back, excited. "Wake up, Gordon! The Fat Controller's given you a surprise. Look!"

Gordon could hardly belive it. Backing towards him were two massive green tenders, and their engine's shape was very like his own. "It's Flying Scotsman!" he gasped. "The Fat Controller's brought him to see me. Oh thank you, Sir!"

Gordon's toot of joy was drowned by Flying Scotsman's as he drew happily alongside.

Next day the two engines were photographed side by side.

"You've changed a lot," smiled Flying Scotsman.

"I had a 'rebuild' at Crewe. They didn't do a proper Doncaster job, of course, but it serves."

"I had a 'rebuild' too, and looked hideous. But my Owner said I was an Extra Special Engine, and made them give me back my proper shape."

'Is that why you have two tenders, being Special?"

"No. You'd hardly believe it, Gordon, but Over There, they've hardly *any coal and water*."

"But surely, every *proper* railway . . . ."

"Exactly. You are lucky, Gordon, to have a Controller who knows how to run railways."

Everyone got on well with Flying Scotsman except Henry. Henry was jealous.

"Tenders are marks of distinction," he complained. "Everybody knows that. Why's he got two?"

"He's famous," explained Duck and Donald. "He was the second to go 100 miles an hour; besides, the Other Railway has no coal and water."

"Pooh!" sniffed Henry. "I can't belive *that*! I never boast," he continued, "but I always work hard enough for two. I deserve another tender for that."

Duck whispered something to Donald.

"Henry," asked Duck innocently, "would you like *my* tenders?"

"Yours!" exclaimed Henry. "What have *you* got to do with tenders?"

"All right," said Duck. "The deal's off. Would you like them Donald?"

'I wudna deprive ye of the honour."

"It *is* a great honour," said Duck, thoughtfully, "but I'm only a tank-engine, so I don't really understand tenders. Perhaps James might . . . ."

"I'm sorry I was rude," said Henry hastily. "How many tenders have you, and when could I have them?"

"Six, and you can have them this evening."

"Six lovely tenders," chortled Henry. "What a splendid sight I'll be! That'll show the others the sort of engine I am!"

Henry was excited. "D'you think it'll be all right?" he asked for the umpteenth time.

"Of course," said Duck. "Just go where I told you, and they'll all be ready."

Meanwhile, word had gone round, and the others waited where they could get a good view. Henry was cheered to the echo when he came, but he wasn't a splendid sight. He had six tenders, true, but they were very old and very dirty. All were filled with boiler sludge!

"Had a good wash-out, Henry?" called a voice. "That's right. You feel a different engine now." Henry was not so sure, but he thought the voice was Gordon's.

## Super Rescue

THE two diesels surveyed the shed. "It's time, 7101," said one, "that we took this railway over."

"Shsh, 199! It's *their* railway, after all."

"Not for long," persisted 199. "Our Controller says, 'Steam engines spoil our Image'."

"Of course we do," snapped Duck. "We show what frauds you are. Call yourselves engines? If anything happens, *you* care nothing for your train. *You* just moan for a fitter. *We* bring it home if only on one cylinder."

"Nothing," boasted 199, "*ever* happens to us. *We* are reliable."

Vulgar noises greeted this.

"How rude!" said 199.

"You asked for it," growled 7101. "Now shut up!"

Next day, Henry was rolling home, tender-first. "I'm a 'failed engine'," he mourned. "Lost my Regulator—Driver says it's jammed wide open, and he can't mend it till I'm cool."

"However," he went on, "I've got steam, and Driver can use my Reverser; but it *would* happen after Duck fooled me with those tenders. Now they'll laugh at me again."

He reached a signalbox and stopped, whistling for a "road".

Opposite the Box, on the "up" line, stood diesel 199 with a train of oil-tankers.

"Worse and worse," thought Henry. "Now 'Old Reliable' will laugh at me, too."

The Signalman came out. "For pity's sake take this Spamcan away. It's failed. The 'Limited' is behind, and all he does is wail for his Fitter."

"Spamcan!" fumed 199. "I'm . . . ."

'Stow it!" snapped the Signalman, "or I'll take my tin-opener to you. Now then!"

199 subsided at this dreadful threat, and Henry pulled the train out of the way. The diesel didn't help. He just sulked.

The "Limited" rushed by with a growl and a roar. Henry gave a chuckle. "Look, Spamcan," he said. "There's your little pal."

The diesel said nothing. He hoped 7101 hadn't noticed.

7101 hadn't noticed. He had troubles of his own. He was cross with his coaches. They seemed to be getting heavier. He roared at them, but it did no good.

Engines have a pump called an Ejector, which draws air out of the train's brake pipes to keep the brakes "off". If it fails, air leaks in and the brakes come "on", gently at first, then harder and harder.

7101's Ejector had failed. The brakes were already "leaking on" while he passed Henry. He struggled on for half-mile before being brought to a stand, growling furiously, unable to move a wheel.

"Well! Well! Well! Did you hear what Signalman said?"

"I thought they'd be laughing at me!" chuckled Henry. "Now, the joke's on them!"

"Moving two 'dead' diesels and their trains?" said his Driver thoughtfully. "That's no joke for a 'failed' engine. D'you think you can do it?"

"I'll have a good try," said Henry with spirit. "Anyway, 7101's better than old Spamcan. He did try and shut him up last night."

"Come on, then," said his Driver. "We mustn't keep the passengers waiting."

"GET MOV – ING YOU!" Henry puffed the sulky diesel into motion, and started to the rescue.

Henry gently buffered up to the express. While the two Drivers talked, his Fireman joined his front brake-pipe to the coaches.

"It's better than we thought, Henry," said his Driver. "The diesel can pull if we keep the brakes 'off'. So the only weight we'll have is Spamcan's goods."

"Whoosh!" said Henry. "That's a mercy." He was, by now, feeling rather puffed.

"Poop poop poopoop! Are you ready?" tooted 7101.

"Peep peep peeeep! Yes I am!' whistled Henry.

So, with 7101 growling in front, and Henry gamely puffing in the middle, the long cavalcade set out for the next Big Station.

Donald and Flying Scotsman were waiting. They cheered as Henry puffed past.

He braked the coaches thankfully; Spamcan and the tankers trailed far behind.

The passengers buzzed out like angry bees; but the Fat Controller told them about Henry, so they forgot to be cross and thanked Henry instead. They called him an Enterprising Engine, and took his photograph.

They were thrilled too, when Flying Scotsman backed down on their train. If the Guard hadn't tactfully "shooed" them to their coaches the train would have started later than ever.

Donald took the "goods". "Return 199 to the Other Railway," ordered the Fat Controller' "I will write my views later."

Henry and 7101 went away together.

"I'm sorry about last night," ventured the diesel.

'That's all right. You did shut 'Old Reliable' up."

"And," said the diesel ruefully, "made a fool of myself today too."

"Rubbish! A failed Ejector might happen to anyone: I'd lost my Regulator."

"You! Failed?" exclaimed the diesel. "And yet . . ." His voice trailed away in admiration.

"Well!" said Henry, "Emergency, you know . Trains *must* get through."

7101 said no more. He had a lot to think about.

## Escape

DOUGLAS had taken the "Midnight Goods" to a station on the Other Railway. He was shunting ready for his return journey, when he heard a faint "Hissssssssssssss".

"That sounds like an engine," he thought.

The "Hisssss" came again. This time, it sounded almost despairing. "Who's there?" he asked.

A whisper came. "Are you a Fat Controller's engine?"

"Aye, and proud of it."

'Thank goodness! I'm Oliver. We're escaping to your railway, but we've run out of coal, and I've no more steam."

"Is it from scrap ye're escaping?"

"Yes."

"Then it's glad I'll be to help ye; but we maun wurrk fast."

Both crews joined in. They took off Oliver's side-rods, wrote out transit labels, and chalked SCRAP everywhere they could. Douglas marshalled Oliver in front of his train. "No time to turrn round,' he panted. "I maun run tender furrst."

"Yoohoo! Yoohoo!" yelled a passing diesel. "A steamer's escaping! Yoohoo!"

Douglas puffed firmly on. "Take no notice," he counselled; but they were stopped before they could clear the station throat.

The Foreman's lamp shone on Oliver. "Aha!" he exclaimed. "A 'Western' engine!" His light flickered further back. "A 'Western' auto-coach, and goods-brake too! You can't take these."

"Can we no!" said Douglas' Driver. "They're all fer uz. See fer yeself."

Douglas' Guard showed him the labels and papers. Oliver's crew, hiding in the coach, hardly dared to breathe.

"Seems in order" said the Foreman grudgingly, "but it's queer."

"Sure, and it is," began the Guard, "but I could tell you queerer . . . ."

"So could I!" interrupted the Foreman. "Right away, Guard."

"A near thing," puffed Douglas with relief.

"We've had worse," smiled Oliver. "We ran at night. Friendly signalmen would pass us from box to box when no trains were about. We got on well till 'Control' heard about a 'mystery train'. Then, they tried to hunt us down."

"What did you do?"

"A signalman let us hide on an old quarry branch. Driver, Fireman and Guard blocked the cutting with rubbish, and levered one of the approach rails away. We stayed there for days, with diesels baying and growling like hounds outside. I was very frightened then."

"Small blame to you," said Douglas feelingly.

Presently they rumbled over the bridge and on to the Fat Controller's Railway.

"We're home! They can't catch ye noo."

"Tell Isabel and Toad please."

Douglas called out the news, and heard a joyful "Tingalinaling! Tingalingaling!" He was surprised.

Oliver chuckled. "That's Isabel," he said. "There is a bell on her you see. She's clever. When we go out together, I pull one way, and push the other. When I pull, I can see ahead. When I push, I can't; so Isabel keeps a good look-out, and rings her bell to talk to me."

"Ye dinna say!" Douglas was impressed.

'Aboot this Toad," he continued. "Is he . . ."

"Haud yer wheesht," said his Driver. "Yon's the Wurrks. We maun slip in unbeknownst, and find a place for Oliver."

Douglas tried hard to be quiet, but the Night Foreman heard them, and had to be told their secret. "I know just the place," he said, and showed them an empty siding nicely hidden away.

Oliver said "Goodbye" and "Thank you", and Douglas puffed away. "Yon's an enterprising engine," he thought. "I won away here with Donald; but I'd've been feared to do it on my own."

## Little Western

DOUGLAS arrived back in time to see Flying Scotsman take his Enthusiasts home.

The Fat Controller said they had all been honoured, and thanked Flying Scotsman and his Owner for their help. "Please tell everyone," he went on, "that whatever happens elsewhere, steam will still be at work here. We shall be glad to welcome all who want to see, and travel behind, *real* engines."

This announcement was greeted with cheers, and Flying Scotsman departed to the strains of "Will ye no come back again?" led, as one might expect, by Donald and Douglas.

At last Douglas could tell his news. They were all excited about it, and agreed that something must be done for Oliver.

"I'm feared," said Donald, "some murdering diesel may creep in, and him there alone, lacking steam even to whistle for help."

"You're right," said James. "He won't be safe till the Fat Controller knows."

"Douglas should tell him at once," said Gordon firmly.

"Is it me speak to the Fat Controller? It's forward he'd think me, and maybe interfering."

"Well, here he is!" said a cheerful voice. "Now, what's this all about?"

Duck broke the awkward silence. "Beg pardon, Sir, but we do need another engine."

"I agree, Duck. That is why I am giving 7101 another chance." Their faces showed such dismay that the Fat Controller had difficulty with his own!

"Sir," ventured Gordon at last. "We had hoped for a *real* engine.

"They," said the Fat Controller gravely, "are rare, and unless one escapes, there's a little hope . . ."

"But, Sirr," burst out Donald, "one *has* . . ."

". . . and, thanks to Douglas, is now at our Works," announced the Fat Controller.

"Sirr," gasped Douglas, "Is there anything ye don't know?"

"More than you think," he laughed.

"Oliver's crew told me all you did, Douglas ...."

"Och, 'Sirr! Ye couldna' see a braw wee engine, and him in trouble, and no do a wheel's turn ...."

"More than 'a wheel's turn', I fancy. Douglas, I'm pleased with you. Oliver, Isabel, and Toad will soon be ours. Oliver and Isabel are just what we need for Duck's Branch Line ...."

Loud cheers greeted this announcement.

".... and Toad wants to be your brakevan, Douglas."

"Thank you, Sirr. I'd hoped for that. He and I'll do brawly together."

That, of course, made everything right. Henry spoke a good word for 7101, and the others gave him a welcome.

He had good manners for a start, so Henry didn't find it hard to teach him our ways. 7101 finds them different from those of the Other Railway, but much more interesting. He is now quite a useful engine.

They teased him at first because of his growls. They said he was like a bear. He still growls, not because he is cross, but because he can't help it. His name, "Bear", has stuck. He likes it.

"It's nicer than just a number," he says. "Having a name means that you really belong."

The Fat Controller soon had Oliver, Isabel and Toad mended and painted in full Great Western colours. Then, he rescued three more "Western" auto-coaches. Two, Alice and Mirabel, he gave to Duck. The third, Dulcie, joined Oliver and Isabel.

Duck and Oliver are happy on their Branch Line. It runs along the coast to the Small Railway. "We *re-open* branches," they boast.

They are very proud of this indeed.

The others laughed at first, and called their Branch, "The Little Western". Duck and Oliver were delighted, and now, no one ever thinks of calling it anything else.

# The Island of Sodor

**Troublesome Engines**
1. Henry meets the elephant in Tidmouth Tunnel, G1
2. The turntable is at Tidmouth, F1
3. Percy runs away from Knapford and stops at Wellsworth, G1, 4

**Percy the Small Engine**
4. The Signal which puzzles Percy, G1
5. Duck takes charge at Tidmouth, F1
6. Newharbour works are at Knapford, G1
7. Harold's airfield, G2
8. Floods, G2

**Duck and the Diesel Engine**
9. Gordon loses his dome on Cronk Viaduct, G6
10. City of Truro runs through to Tidmouth, F1
11. Duck and Diesel quarrel at Tidmouth, F1
12. The trucks break away at Maron, G5
13. The barber's shop is at Crosby, G2

**Main Line Engines**
14. China Clay beds, 15
15. Bees get loose at Tidmouth, F1
16. Gordon switched to branch at Suddery junction, G4
17. Edward's exploit on train returning from Brendam to Tidmouth, J5

**Enterprising Engines**
18. Henry gets his tenders at Tidmouth, F1
19. Oliver rescued by Douglas at Barrow, E13
20. Henry's "super rescue" between Kelsthorpe Road and Cronk, 9, G6.
21. "The Little Western" is Duck's Arlesburgh Branch, G1, E2.

This volume first published in Great Britain in 1985 by
Kaye & Ward Ltd  an imprint of William Heinemann Ltd
for W.H. Smith & Son Ltd under the title Selected Engine Stories

This edition published in 1989 by
Treasure Press
Michelin House
81 Fulham Road
London
SW3 6RB

ISBN 1 85051 461 5

Produced by Mandarin Offset
Printed in Hong Kong